ELEPHANT CHILD

ROARING GOOD READS

Collins

An imprint of HarperCollinsPublishers

Roaring Good Reads will fire the imagination of all young readers – from short stories for children just starting to read on their own, to first chapter books and short novels for confident readers.

www.roaringgoodreads.co.uk

Also by Mary Ellis

The Arctic Fox
Lily Dragon

More Roaring Good Reads from Collins

ELEPHANT CHILD

Mary Ellis

ILLUSTRATED BY

Kady MacDonald Denton

An imprint of HarperCollins*Publishers*

Acknowledgements:
With thanks to Shola Amifonoshe.
The wonderful work and books of Iain and Oria Douglas-Hamilton and
their tireless struggle to save the lives of elephants. *Among the Elephants*
(1975) *Battle for the Elephants* (1992). *Things Fall Apart* by Chinua Achebe.

▲
▼

First published in Great Britain in hardback by Collins 2001
First published in paperback by Collins 2003
Collins is an imprint of HarperCollins*Publishers* Ltd
77-85 Fulham Palace Road, Hammersmith,
London, W6 8JB

The HarperCollins website address is:
www.**fire**and**water**.com

2

Text copyright © Mary Ellis 2001
Illustrations by Kady MacDonald Denton 2001

ISBN 0 00 712820 7

Printed and bound in England by Clays Ltd, St Ives plc

for Tom and Kim, with love always

In memory of
Marcy and Allistair

CHAPTER 1

SHOLA

This isn't just my story, it never was, it is Shola's too. She is my sister and I have loved her from the moment I saw my father carry her in his arms from the plane. She was exhausted and half-starved but my mongoose, Daisy, snuggled next to her and Shola's face lit up.

My parents had been out as usual in the plane, researching the movement of elephants in Bakuli National Park, our home in Africa. They were at the far end of the reserve, where the escarpment meets the white shores of the soda lake in a dramatic sweep of acacia woodland. They had seen one of the elephant families acting strangely. They circled in the plane

and landed to get a closer look. Although the elephants were used to my parents, they moved away. It was the plane that had worried them. Sala, the elephant leader, fanned out her ears in a mock charge. My parents crept forwards. They had spotted something in amongst the bushes and wild flowers. It was the body of a child. It was Shola.

From Shola's faltering description my parents are now sure that the elephants had treated her like one of their own young. They had touched her repeatedly with their trunks. Without this tenderness, Shola would most certainly have died.

I remember listening to my parents talking to her as she lay curled up in our camp. She was taking food slowly and hugging Daisy. She had apparently been walking for many days on her own before finding the elephants.

"Maybe the orphan of refugees," my mother had muttered. That was all we ever found out. Although Shola spoke Swahili, my parents discovered that "Shola" means "joyful" in the language of a far-off tribe.

Shola had seven tiny little lines, tribal marks, cut into her chest and back, her arms and the top of her head. I remember my mother hugging us both close to her and saying:

"You see, Shola's mother put these little marks, *chale*, on her for protection. Sala and the elephants took care of her and now she's safe with us."

Shola was about five when my parents found her. I was four and at last I had a sister. Someone my own size to catch beetles and dragonflies with. Someone to play and splash with me in the soft sands of the Wimbo riverbed. My mother said that "Wimbo" meant "song" in Swahili and she imagined it had been named after the call of the elephants. Every evening we watched them follow the impala down to the river in the gathering dusk. As the first stars appeared in the huge African sky, I made a wish that Shola could stay for ever. Our family now felt complete.

CHAPTER 2

A TAPPING

No one ever came for Shola. Her story was written up in the newspapers and passed by word of mouth through the neighbouring villages. People would arrive quite suddenly to meet her, "the child saved by the elephants". They already thought my father and mother's life was so close to the elephants as to be reckless, but they agreed Shola fitted right into our family group. And so, she stayed with us.

I had been brought up to think of elephants as kind and gentle. My parents knew every one of the six hundred elephants in the park by sight and had names for all of them. Elephants live in families just as we do; they love and care for each other. Sala, the eldest female, was the leader of the family group my parents watched and researched most closely.

Although nearly all the elephants were used to my parents' presence, only one elephant was actually curious enough to come over and greet them. This was Lulu. She was Sala's youngest daughter and easy to recognise because she had a flower-shaped tear in one of her ears. But Dad rewarded her curiosity with figs and pomegranates. When my parents introduced me to her, she extended her trunk to my outstretched hand. I felt a rushing like a warm breeze on my palm. It is a sensation like no other and I was amazed. With Shola, Lulu actually touched her cheek with her trunk. Lulu's huge, beautiful eyes closed for a moment as though she too was sealing this precious moment. An elephant never forgets a friend and she had been there the day Shola was found.

I know now that children have so many different realities, but this was ours: we lived on the research camp my parents had built for themselves out of stones from the waterfall close by. Baboons, sitting above the falls, watched as Mum and Dad made their home and brought me and then Shola to join them. Our kitchen, with its primitive oven, was a little round hut further up the hill.

Shola, Daisy and I shared a sleeping hut and slept together on a mattress on the floor. In the wet season our room was filled with the sweet smell of jasmine and the sound of the distant rumble of elephants. We ate on a covered veranda that ran between our and Mum and Dad's sleeping huts. We'd helped to make the sofa and chairs that we sat on out of boxes and brilliantly coloured material bought from the village market.

Each day we would set off along the elephant trails in the Waterstream Forest. We would wander barefoot in magical sunlit corridors of moss trodden down by generations of elephants. We'd climb trees and then make our own camps from fallen logs on the forest floor.

Mali, the park ranger who worked with my parents, was our special friend.

He was very tall and calm and nothing we did ever surprised him. He said he'd grown up watching and learning about animals and we were just another set of cubs he'd have to keep an eye on. He told us the names of plants and of how to track animals by their spoor. He taught us not to befriend scorpions and reminded us constantly that we had to keep an eye out for the mangy lions that rested in the trees. Best of all he taught us to imitate the call of the nightjar.

At night our heads were filled with characters from the stories Mum and Dad would tell us underneath the largest fig tree next to our camp. On one such evening Dad had Daisy asleep in his lap. Mali was there and also Elder and Paula, our friends who were vets for the National Parks. Their son, Tatu, was our age. We were eating soup and chapati. Dad was telling us about the Bushmen whom he had met in the desert years before:

"They talked with a strange clicking sound. They spoke of a tapping that comes from listening to thoughts that come from deep within our hearts. We all have this tapping, they said, if only we listened to it."

That moment stands out in my mind because now I wonder if I had felt a tapping in my heart that told me all this precious happiness was fleeting, and that soon it would be wrenched from us.

CHAPTER 3

〰〰〰

THE END

It was a shock when, at the age of six, we realised that our parents and Mali could no longer be our teachers. We had to go to school. They let Shola wait for me to be six and then we went together.

In a small whitewashed building, in the village of Matambilli, Mrs B. set about educating me, Shola and Tatu. She was an imperious woman with a heart of gold who believed in a sound grounding in numbers and grammar. She established this by leading her class to the market to count pawpaws and melons on the stalls run by her former pupils. A necessary part of the lesson was tasting the fruit and then playing a game of stones in the sand.

"Music is as important to life as breathing," she would declare, and suddenly burst into song. She taught us to play drums and rattles that we made ourselves.

〰〰〰〰〰

Three years later, at about the time when Mrs B. was teaching us algebra in the marketplace, Mum and Dad agreed to do an elephant count in the neighbouring

Senvali National Park. Every day, after dropping us at school, Mum and Dad would get into their little plane and set off over the Senvali. At the end of the day, our hearts would quicken at the sound of their plane returning. Then all the joy that they carried would tumble into our evening.

It was June 12th. Elder was driving us home. Shola was making Tatu and me laugh. She was hugging Elder's dog, Teddy, and trying to catch pods as we drove under the sausage trees. Shola and I had a new book to start reading that night: *Tom's Midnight Garden*. I knew it was Mum's favourite.

We heard the sound of a plane engine and begged Elder to let us run up to the landing strip to greet Mum and Dad. Mali would already be there. Elder let us down and Tatu came too.

"I'll follow," cried Elder. He was waiting for some giraffes to cross the track in front of the car.

"Sala's family will already be at the Wimbo," called Shola. "Let's get Mama and Baba to come for a swim."

We ran up to the landing strip only to realise that it was not Mum and Dad's plane that was landing. The next bit I remember as if in slow motion. A tall man in a dark suit climbed down from this strange plane.

"The Police Commissioner," muttered Mali. He and Elder rushed forward to meet him. I bent down to hug Teddy.

"Feel his ears, Shola, they're so soft."
Shola didn't answer. She was staring
straight ahead at Elder and Mali. Elder
had turned towards us. The colour had
drained from his face. Mali crouched
down next to us, taking each of our hands.
I saw tears coming from his eyes. Even
then I didn't understand.

"It's Mama and Baba, isn't it?" said
Shola in a voice I'd never heard her use
before.

"Their plane came down... it's all
wrong," gasped Mali at last. "Their
shadows... gone."

I couldn't see Shola any more. I couldn't
hear the noise of the African evening. I
couldn't even feel my body.

"MUMMY... DADDY," I screamed.

CHAPTER 4

✕✕✕✕

A YEAR

A whole year has gone by and today, as I sit in this little plane going back to Bakuli, I think for the first time I feel alive again. The engine is roaring, there are pink flamingos and white pelicans on Lake Maribu below me and my heart is beating with excitement.

The terrible thing about being a child with no parents is that strangers make decisions for you. Something inside me stopped when Mum and Dad were taken from us. At first I don't think I was aware of anything much except that Shola was gone as well.

Mum and Dad had never formally adopted Shola. No doubt they would have done in time, but there hadn't been a reason to do so. It was all just understood. Then, on the day their plane crashed, all that seemed to matter to everyone was paperwork. Shola was to stay with Paula and Elder. I was taken, in a daze, to my next of kin, my aunt and uncle in England.

They lived in a large red brick house in a long street of red brick houses. My aunt and uncle were very kind to me but they felt so remote; I was suspended like a spectator in the unfamiliar world around me. When I looked out of the window of my room, I saw only as far as the moon on the rooftops opposite. It was suffocating. I closed my eyes and tried to see the sun setting on the horizon of the Africa I'd left behind. My cousins would hold me helplessly when I woke up sobbing for Shola and for Daisy.

One such night I couldn't sleep and I went and sat at the top of the stairs. I heard my aunt saying:

"You cannot take a child from everything he loves. No wonder he screams at night. He's lost his parents, his sister and everything that was precious to him."

"But what choice have we got?" said my uncle. "We are his guardians, he belongs with us now. We know little about Africa, even less of Shola."

"We knew Marcy and Allistair loved Shola as a daughter," said my aunt firmly. "We know Leo loves her as a sister and that is all we need to know. Leo needs to go home to her and to Africa if he's going to get through this. As his guardians we must do what is right for him and what Marcy and Allistair would have wanted for their two children."

"Isn't it too much to ask of Paula and Elder?" said my uncle.

"They say they want him to be with them," insisted my aunt. "It's selfish of us to consider anything else. Even if it is just for a while. You must see that it can't be right for Leo to stay here."

To hear my inner feelings explained brought a rush of tears to my eyes. I was dizzy with hope. I crept back into my room and picked up the photo of Mum and Dad standing in the Waterstream Forest, smiling at me. I knew then, at that moment, that they were still with me after all, watching over me, deep in my heart. Every day they would always be there for me. It was a tremendous and comforting certainty.

CHAPTER 5

✖✖✖✖✖

SILENCE

At last I saw that familiar ribbon of forest and grassland nestled beside the white shoreline of our lake.

"My home... quick... IT'S OVER THERE!" I yelled, the echo uplifting my heart to bursting point. "HURRY! Oh, please hurry!" The pilot was laughing and

we dropped, bumping into the hot air, flying low over the Wimbo River towards the strip. The little plane landed and slowly taxied to a standstill. Together we opened the door and all the intoxicating smells of home blew into the cabin. Through the heat haze a cluster of figures hurried towards us.

"MALI, PAULA, ELDER, OH! TATU!" I jumped into their outstretched arms. "TEDDY!" I screamed as he fell upon me, knocking me over, all licks and paws. We were laughing and scolding and crying at the same time. At last I was with people who could look at me and see the real me.

"But Shola," I said, "where is she?"

"At the camp," said Mali. "She's finding beetles for you to give Daisy, but Leo, you should know..." The wind caught his words. I'd already started running.

"I'll find her! It's OK!"

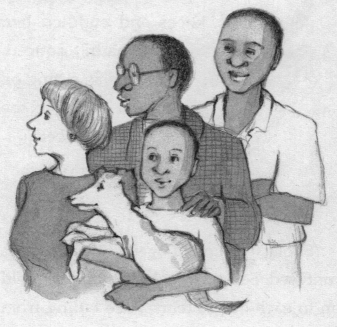

"SHOLA!" I yelled as I ran down the hill to the Wimbo River. Each tree was as familiar to me as though I'd never been away – confirmation that all this still existed and hadn't been a dream.

It was Daisy who saw me first. She'd picked up my scent and came haring towards me. She nibbled and purred as I fell to my knees and cuddled her. Shola hadn't noticed. She was sitting on a rock in the riverbed.

"Shola!" I shouted again. She stood up, confused. Seeing me, she ran and we held on to each other. Tears were falling from our eyes. I can't remember how long we held on to each other. Shola didn't speak but held my hand tightly.

"We won't be separated again, Sho, I promise." Shola nodded.

Teddy came bounding over and Daisy jumped inside my shirt. We were together again. For one brief second I imagined maybe none of the nightmare had happened after all. That Mum and Dad would come out of the camp door and call us over. But I knew they wouldn't.

I couldn't even hear the rumble of elephants, which seemed strange, as you could always hear them at this time of day. Shola was showing me something she had written in the sand.

Leo, I can't speak any more. I thought I'd never see you again. I thought you'd gone like Mama and Baba.

I looked at her, not understanding. Shola looked down at Teddy.

Tatu was beside us. "She can't speak, Leo. That's what Mali wanted to say. Ever since the accident Shola can't speak. It's a kind of shock isn't it, Shola? The doctors told us that. Her voice has just gone."

"Will it come back?" I asked Shola. She smiled and shrugged and kissed Daisy. She seemed as mystified as I was. Tatu answered for her.

"It could. There's no reason why it can't."

"Where are Sala's family, where are the elephants?" I said suddenly. "Aren't they usually here by now?" Even in the dry season when the Wimbo River was just a trickle of water, the elephants came to splash, play and make wells. The rains had come late and I could see the river still had plenty of water. Shola took a stick and wrote:

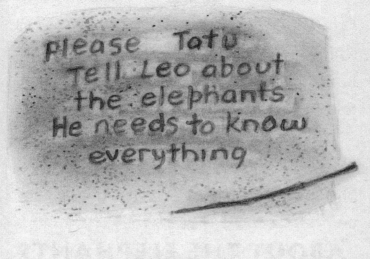

Please Tatu
Tell Leo about
the elephants
He needs to know
everything

CHAPTER 6

〰〰〰

ABOUT THE ELEPHANTS

Tatu looked at the ground. He seemed reluctant to speak. I noticed how much taller and skinnier Tatu had grown since I'd been away. Shola was hugging her knees and waiting for him to begin... he was her voice. She too was skinnier and although she laughed and smiled, her eyes didn't dance like I remembered. Her silence was bewildering. I put out my hand to touch the ring of carved black and red beads around her neck. They were our mother's beads, she had worn them all the time. They must have been found in amongst the wreckage and had seemed like a gift to Shola.

"Since you've been gone, Leo," began Tatu, "something terrible has happened. A lot of the elephants have been killed; many, many elephants. At the last count Mali found only one hundred and eighty-one alive."

"Killed," I interrupted in horror. "But how... why? How could anyone hurt the elephants?"

"Poachers," said Tatu in disgust, and he spat in the dust. "Thieves who kill elephants for the money they can make by selling their tusks. Do you remember your father telling us how ivory sells in certain countries for large amounts of money?"

I did remember. I remembered he and my mother sitting up late, writing letters to different organisations. I remember Mum trying to explain it to us:

"In Africa, some countries aren't allowed to sell ivory as it's led to the killing of so many elephants. But a few countries are still allowed to sell it because they have large elephant populations and they say their ivory comes from elephants that have died naturally. The terrible truth is that as long as people can get money from ivory poaching in even one part of Africa, poaching will carry on all over Africa and elephants will die," she said.

"So when they get your letter they will stop allowing it… it will be made illegal everywhere," said Shola. My dad stood up and kissed us both.

"If only children could teach the world what they see so clearly... grown-ups make it all too complicated."

What would they have thought as they sat there, with the moths dancing in the glow of the gas lamp, if they'd known that in a year only one hundred and eighty-one of their six hundred elephants would still be alive. Tears came to my eyes and I felt again the ache of loss.

"Can't we stop them?" I cried. Anger was welling up inside me. "Bakuli is a park, it's their home, it's a sanctuary for the elephants. They came here trusting us to take care of them. They are our friends."

"The poachers are like armies," said Tatu. "I saw them with guns and spears. It took ages to get help. Mali's done

everything he can but he desperately needs more rangers to patrol the park. It's gone a lot quieter now since the rangers arrived. A lot of the elephants left are the younger ones."

"Orphans like us," Shola wrote carefully in the sand.

"Not Sala?" Naively I clung to a hope that she might have been spared. Shola shook her head. "And Lulu?" I said, the full horror as yet impossible to comprehend.

"No one knows," said Tatu. "A ranger thought he spotted her five months ago."

Later that afternoon, on Paula and Elder's little veranda, Mali spoke to me.

"Leo, sometimes I think it is as though our small corner of the earth has been touched by a terrible cloud of sadness. Your return is the beginning of hope and light."

"How can they do it, Mali? How can they kill our elephants? I did not know that people had such cruelty in them."

Mali shook his head.

"Where are the other elephants now, Mali? They didn't come to the river."

"In the Utenzi Cloud Forest. They hide there now. It is safer for them in amongst the dense canopy of leaves. They say that when an elephant is angry, the earth shakes. There have been days when, after the shooting has stopped, I have felt the ground tremble beneath me."

CHAPTER 7

∞∞∞

APHONIA

There is a rope swing at the bottom of Paula and Elder's garden. They tied it there when Tatu was a baby. When we were younger, only Shola could climb on to it by herself. Tatu and I would watch longingly as she'd jump on from the little bank and swing gaily across to the stone wall.

It was so clear that night, we stayed outside by the swing, taking it in turns to fly through the air. We saw the sun set over the Utenzi Cloud Forest where our elephants were now hiding. In the distance, as punctual as the chimes of a grandfather clock, the lions roared to greet the darkness. The bats swooped above us, announcing the arrival of the starry night sky.

"If Lulu's alive, we must find her," I said, stopping suddenly. "Mum and Dad would want us to." Shola nodded. I missed her words.

Later on, when Shola was helping Elder and Tatu to tend to the sick genet cats, I found Paula.

"Paula, if Shola's happy today, why can't her speech come back? I miss her even though I am with her. It is as though a part of her is still far away." Paula sat down next to me and brushed my hair absentmindedly.

"Leo, I've read all I can about Shola's condition. It is called Aphonia. I can only explain it like this: when your mum and dad died, the shock shut down the part of Shola's brain that controls her speech. And, of course, we still don't know what sadness is inside her from the time the elephants found her. There's nothing wrong with her speech, but the fact that it doesn't work is like an outward sign of her inner shock. It will come back, we think, but only when she is ready. Shola is happy today, Leo, but we must be patient. The brain is a mysterious and sensitive part of us.

"Shola has been like a nomad since you left; even though we have been made her guardians, it's only recently that we've got her to stay with us. At first she would only sleep in your rondavel by the river with Daisy. Mali's mother would go there to watch over her. We never knew where she would turn up to eat. Sometimes it was at Mrs B.'s or sometimes at Mali's home, or with us. It's only since she knew you were coming that she has slept here."

Shola and Tatu had decorated our room with "WELCOME HOME LEO" signs, written in silver pen on large leaves strung together. Paula and Elder had unpacked my bag. There was a candle by each of our beds. Daisy was already curled up on my pillow. Shola was in her nightie and was writing something. I kissed Daisy. I still couldn't believe that I was back with them again. Shola made her note into a paper aeroplane and flew it over to my bed.

"Why did they leave us behind?" she had written in her careful script.

"But they haven't, Sho," I exclaimed. "They're still with us. Mum and Dad said they'd always protect you, protect both of us. They are, I can feel it."

Shola wrote another note:

> Can you read us Tom's Midnight Garden, Leo. I've kept it. We were going to read it, weren't we? It was Mama's favourite.

So we sat on my bed and I began to read. Daisy sat at our feet, tickling us when she squirmed.

We must have fallen asleep as I read, because I was woken with a start and realised I'd been dreaming of Lulu. She was there so clearly, in amongst the trees with Kim and Ashanti, her cousins. I called out to her and woke myself up.

Teddy came padding in from Tatu's room to see what the noise was. Shola and Daisy slept on.

"Tomorrow," I promised myself. "Tomorrow I'll ask Mali if we can search for Lulu. We've got to know where she and the other elephants are... if they're alive."

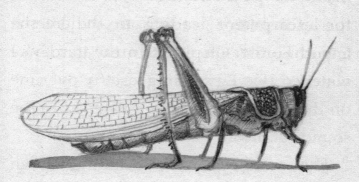

CHAPTER 8

GRASSHOPPERS

I was the first up. After being away, the dawn of this new African day was all the more precious to me. I crept out in my pyjamas to look for grasshoppers for Daisy. They are much easier to catch early in the morning when their wings are heavy with dew.

Paula and Elder's little house stood just inside the park boundaries, at the foot of the escarpment leading to the Utenzi Cloud Forest. Once out in the garden, I watched two Egyptian geese fly over me on their way to the lake. I listened to the sounds of Bakuli's animals stirring.

The monkeys were climbing down from their resting places to warm themselves in the sun, chattering gleefully like children.

The house began to stir too, and Daisy and Shola came running out to catch grasshoppers with me. Tatu said we were all going to school; Mrs B. was waiting for us. I hadn't a moment to lose on my education, which she feared would have suffered during my year in England.

Elder brought us cereal and bread under the umbrella tree. Daisy was so full of grasshoppers that she'd fallen asleep on my lap.

Mali was taking us to school as he had to go into town anyway. When he arrived, we ran into the house to say goodbye. On the table were our lunch boxes. The memories came flooding back. Mum had found some wooden chocolate boxes from Belgium; the scent of chocolate had lingered on for days. She'd painted and varnished them for us with our names.

Mine had a picture of Daisy on it and lots of brightly-coloured insects. Shola's was painted with lions and elephants. We'd always been so proud of them. I kissed Paula.

"Thank you for finding them."

"It was Shola, Leo, she found them and brought them here."

Teddy had to stay at home. Even though Mrs B. pretended she didn't allow animals in school, we knew she had a soft spot for Daisy. She was sometimes allowed in the classroom, as long as she slept all day in the shafts of hot sunlight that fell on the windowsill next to the globe.

As we climbed into Mali's jeep, I blurted out the question I'd been wanting to ask since yesterday.

"Mali, would you take us, er… not now, I mean… maybe tomorrow…"

"Take you where?" said Mali, confused.

"Would you take us up the escarpment to the Utenzi Cloud Forest to look for Lulu?" We'd reached the point where the road ran along the edge of the lake. Zebra and wildebeest wandered near the shore. Mali paused.

"What's wrong, Mali?"

"It's only that you sound so like your father, but yes, we will go tomorrow if Paula and Elder agree. The forest is huge and the escarpment is thickly wooded, so we may find it a difficult journey."

"But we've got to try, haven't we, Mali?"

As we drove down the dusty school road we could hear the sound of children already singing our anthem.

When we ran into our classroom everyone clapped and Mrs B. forgot to look strict. She ran forward and clasped me to her large round body. Then, readjusting her brilliantly-coloured turban, she waved me to an empty desk and continued to sing. I was admonished with a look when I tried to talk to one of my friends. I noticed how she quickly gave Shola a drum to play. She, too, was understanding of her silence.

Mrs B. never missed an opportunity for a science lesson that related to real life. That afternoon we helped to carry stones along a dusty track; we were rebuilding a nearby well. At the end of the day I stood in front of the whole school and told them about my year in England.

After school Mrs B. took us back to her house and filled us with sweet pomegranates and baked figs. She talked about the "crime" that Shola and I had ever been separated by no-good solicitors and their paperwork. Sho kissed Mrs B. on the cheek.

"...and kisses are nice, Shola," said Mrs B., "but it's your words I need now, my girl!"

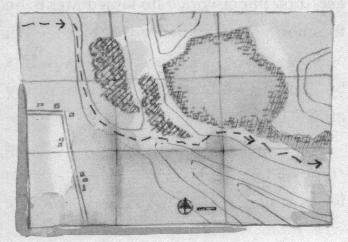

CHAPTER 9

〰〰〰

A PILGRIMAGE

"My tapping is telling us to go," I explained to Paula. We were feeding the genet cats milk from a bottle. "If we can find Lulu and the others then we'll be carrying on for Mum and Dad. The elephants are part of our family. Maybe they are wondering where we are? Like them we've lost our parents, so in some way we all need to be together again."

"A pilgrimage," said Paula thoughtfully. "It's like a pilgrimage."

Shola had gone with Mali to pick up some detailed maps of the escarpment leading to the Utenzi Cloud Forest. We were going the next morning.

Paula and Elder always treated us with trust and spoke to us honestly. I think it was because they felt they were looking after us for Mum and Dad. They understood that Shola and I knew about grown-up sadness. I was grateful to them for this, but there was one question I still had to ask.

"Paula, Mali said that the poachers had killed the older elephants, but why were the little ones spared?"

Paula hugged her genet cat closer to her. "The older elephants have the largest tusks. Worse still is that the poachers know the older elephants protect their young. If they sense danger, the elephant elders form a circle to protect their young.

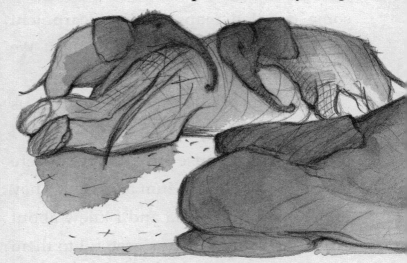

So the poachers break branches to encourage the elephants to form this protective circle. Then they open fire on them, leaving only the orphans standing alive. The orphan elephants try desperately to get their elders to stand again, for they are lost without them."

Paula shivered and stood up, putting the little genet cats into a basket lined with her jumper. "Don't let's talk of this now, Leo. You'll be leaving at first light;

Mali's staying here tonight so you can make an early start. Elder's made up a picnic for you. Oh! and I'm sorry but Tatu can't come with you. He's got to come with us to see his aunt and uncle and the cousins in Shelici. But we'll be back before nightfall to hear all about your adventure."

Mali, Shola and I looked carefully over the maps. They'd been painted by my mother, with notes and arrows scribbled on them by Dad.

"That's what I remember," said Mali. "All along there... the rock face is too steep for the elephants to find a path through to the Utenzi Cloud Forest. But here, underneath Kumomesha Hill is the Utenzi Waterfall. If I remember rightly, there are elephant trails leading gradually up through gullies into the forest. One route only. We must make for the waterfall. The vegetation is thick so we will have to leave the jeep and make our way through the elephant trails on foot. So wear your strong shoes Little Lion – no bare feet," he added, smiling.

We were both awake at five. Excitement tingled through me. We hurried into our clothes, kissed a sleeping Daisy goodbye and went out to the Land Rover.

The moon still hung in the early morning darkness, casting a pathway over the garden. A lizard lay frozen against the kitchen wall. Mali was loading the picnic and it was Teddy who was sitting enthusiastically in the driver's seat, his tail wagging.

"No, Ted," I said as Sho climbed in to get him. "You've got to go with Tatu, and anyway, you might not like it up there." Then we saw the first chink of the deep red sunrise, and a flock of birds on the lake rose to greet the new day.

"Come on," said Mali. "We should be gone. We must chase the dawn as well."

"See you at sunset, Teddy," I called. "Look after Tatu for us."

In a cloud of dust and the crunching of stones, we were off.

CHAPTER 10

HOPE

Our journey took us past Pofu Hot Springs
and along the dusty road track to where
the escarpment touches the shores of Lake
Bakuli. Hundreds of buffalo, giraffe and
impala were silhouetted in the sunrise.
They roamed freely before the quivering
veil of African heat descended upon them.

Mali took the car a short way up the escarpment and then stopped.

"It's footsteps from here, Little Lion. The whistling thorns are telling me we cannot drive any further." He gave us each a small backpack to put on and took a huge one for himself.

Shola had already started on a track that wound up the hill through the spiky wild sisal. As we entered a narrow tunnel through thick undergrowth, I stopped sharply.

"Look! Rhino droppings." They were fresh and unmistakable. So too were the thick, three-toed rhino hoof marks that Shola and Mali found in the dust.

"Shout and whoop now," called Mali loudly. "Warn them of our approach... normally they make way for noisy human beings." All the same, Mali's and my whoops were tremulous as we could only see a few metres ahead of us.

Shola was the first to step out into the grassy riverside glade below the Utenzi Waterfall. A cool breeze came from the water. Anxious to rest after the earlier tension, we were about to sit down when the all-too-familiar crashing of trees reached our ears. Goose pimples scurried down my back.

"*Tembo*," said Mali. Sho grabbed my hand.

"Yes, elephants, Sho, elephants!" I whispered.

Hidden behind a bush we watched, captivated, as a group of elephants made their stately progress down to the opposite riverbank. Like a pack of old friends they rumbled as they walked, taking care to watch over each other. How could anyone ever want to harm them?

I was overwhelmed with the urge to get closer, but we knew that their trust in man could have been destroyed. Thankfully the wind would carry our scent away from the elephants, since now it would only signal fear.

One by one the elephants dropped their trunks into the water and drank deeply. One of them had found a desert fig tree and shook it so that the ripe fruit fell to the ground. The others joined in, sharing it.

Desperately I searched for familiar markings and then I saw the chink in one of their tails.

"Look Mali, Shola… it's Maya! That tail! There couldn't be another one like it!" We'd seen Maya when she was born. She had a funny little bend in her tail. Mum and Dad had taken us out one afternoon and, to our surprise, we'd come upon her being born. We'd named her Maya after Shola's Indian doll. Maya had been part of Nisha's family. They had often moved closely with Sala's family group.

"There's no sign of Angel or Nisha," I said.

"No," whispered Mali. "They were taken by the poachers. They were identified. Maya must have joined up with other orphans."

"Take Lulu our love, Maya. Please, if you can," I whispered. I hoped that my words could turn to rumbles in the enchantment of this glade.

One by one, the elephants moved away and we waded through the river. We climbed up the interlocking trails after them. Back came the old excitement we'd felt with Mum and Dad as we trod in trails worn out by generations of elephants.

A carpet of sunshine opened up ahead
of us, as we reached a meadow of brightly-
coloured flowers. The elephants seemed to
have disappeared into the bush. Under the

green coolness of a mgiri tree, we relaxed and dropped our guard.

All too late I spotted a rhino feeding in a nearby thicket. In that split second it had turned towards us. Its huge leathery face looked menacing and angry.

"Run," I cried to Mali and Sho at the top of my voice. "RUN! The rhino, it's coming for us!"

CHAPTER 11

〰〰

RHINO

Mali grabbed us.

"That way, you run that way!" he shouted in the fiercest voice I had ever heard. "Remember, run up the hill!"

We ran. I felt the ground thundering with hooves, fear dragged at my feet and thorns tore at my t-shirt, but I clung to

Shola's hand. We ran as fast as we could. As fast as I'd ever run.

Shola was quicker than me, sometimes I felt her pulling me on. We daren't look round until Shola stopped and crouched down. She felt the ground and shook her head.

"What, Sho?" I said, gasping for breath. She put her fingers to her lips and I too felt the hot dry ground and listened carefully. There was no movement, no rhino on our tail.

"It's gone... we're OK!" I said, astonished. "We're safe." But Mali was nowhere in sight. A gust of wind blew tantalisingly across the bush, teasing us with a ripple of movement.

"Mali," I shouted. "Mali, are you there?"

Shola had climbed up a nearby tree and I scrambled up next to her. We looked out over the escarpment. We could see the lake, breathtaking and bejewelled in the sunlight beyond, but no sign of Mali or the rhino.

"He sent us a different way, Sho, I know he did, and the rhino followed him downhill."

"MALI," I shouted again. "MALI!"

We started off down the hill. Nothing could ever happen to Mali, he was invincible to us.

"We'll go back to the mgiri tree, Sho, that's the best thing." Shola was already ahead of me. When we got to the tree she was searching for something and then she showed me.

"The rhino tracks. Sho, that's it! We'll follow them if we can." Countless times we had tracked elephants and impala with Mali as our instructor. We had never thought that one day we'd be searching for Mali and that our game would become a desperate reality. All the time his words echoed in my head:

"Little Lion, don't forget that the animal you are tracing could be anywhere close by, just watching and waiting."

We followed the rhino tracks further down the meadow. Any tracks from Mali's shoes must have been churned up by the rhino's thundering hooves. Shola looked at me, her eyes wide with fear.

"Mali!" I shouted. "MALI, ARE YOU THERE?"

Shola saw it first – Mali's backpack, the strap broken, lying in a bush.

"Mali, Mali." I whispered it now, as fear tightened my throat. We crept past the bush and there he lay. Our relief was brief because Mali lay so still. His eyes were closed. Shola held his hand and I called his name urgently again. This time, very reluctantly, his eyes opened.

"Shola, Little Lion, you are here," his eyes flickered, closed, and opened again.

"It's all right, little ones... I fell... it kicked me with its foot... I'm lucky. I'm just broken somewhere. If I can have a minute. I'll be OK..." His words tailed off.

CHAPTER 12

∞∞∞∞

THE WARNING

Shola ran back to the bush for Mali's backpack and dragged it over. Taking the water bottle, she poured a few trickles into Mali's mouth. His lips were pale and blue.

"Shola, it's my leg... he knocked me to one side. I think maybe it's..." he paused and his next words came in a murmur

"…maybe it's broken." He closed his eyes.

"Yes," I pleaded, willing him to continue, but his breathing had become regular and he slept once more.

The cicadas sang oppressively in the afternoon heat.

"It's good for Mali to sleep, isn't it, Sho?" I whispered, remembering Mrs B.'s first-aid lessons. Shola put her hands on Mali's forehead just as Dad used to when we were ill.

"Make a wish, sweetheart," he'd say, "and Kupona, the healer of body and soul, will go to work."

We needed to protect Mali from the sun. We started to unpack the contents of his backpack. Three emergency blankets that looked like tin foil were our solution. We used one of the blankets and four branches from an acacia tree to make a little tent over Mali, with a roll of juniper grass as a pillow.

Mali's gun was lying on the ground beside him. If the rhino returned, or a lion came prowling near, we knew we might have to use it. The radio had been crushed in Mali's fall. It was useless. Shola wrote me a note:

"Paula and Elder will be back by nightfall. If we aren't back they'll come looking for us. They will know something's wrong and they know where to look for us." The hope that there would be a safe ending to this adventure calmed our fears a little.

"We'll surprise Mali and cook the supper on his stove," I said. The backpack had revealed a small treasure-trove of food.

Mali slept on, muttering feverishly at times. We lit the portable gas stove. We mixed rice and sardines with bright red peppers. As the smell of cooking reached Mali, he opened his eyes.

"A feast, well done, little cubs. Very soon they'll come for us. I promise." I gave him more water and a green pill from the first-aid box labelled PAIN RELIEF. Shola came with a spoonful of our "wild bush risotto". Mali held her hand. Beads of perspiration clung to his forehead, but he was shivering too.

"I'll taste it a little later, Shola. When we've lit the candles. Go on, little cubs, eat quickly yourselves. You need your strength."

For a moment I wondered if Mali would survive until help came.

"Mali," I whispered. "I could run back to the jeep and drive it to get help. I've driven it before. I know what to do. Shola would stay here." Mali's face clouded and was full of distress. He growled:

"NO, Little Lion, NO… we stay together. Do not even talk of it. It is my mistake that I am like this. I cannot lose you as well. We might never see you again… now go on, eat, and sing me one of Mrs B.'s ballads."

By the time we'd eaten, stoned dates for pudding and made hot chocolate, Mali was sleeping again. He looked peaceful once more. Shola was standing, looking down the escarpment. The sun cast a soft glow on the tops of the trees and the mountains beyond our lake. It was dusk already.

"Here's your chocolate, Sho," I called. But Shola didn't move.

"What is it, Sho?" She turned to me with her fingers to her lips. When I stood next to her I could feel it too. Had we been visitors to this part of the world we would have been overwhelmed by the sounds of African animals and birds heralding another sunset. Lions, baboons, geese and herons united in a captivating chorus. But something else more portentous was in this sound.

The birds sang at a new and feverish pitch. There was a desperation to this tune, as though they were courting such beauty for the last time. I had only heard this once before when I was little.

"Remember what Baba said?" Shola wrote quickly on her notepad. "Remember this sound, it means the bush is warning us of a danger."

"There's something out there, Sho, isn't there? Look! Above us!" A baboon gazed out, as we did, over the valley. The bleak and mournful cry of the isala bird came from a clump of thorns nearby. We knew from our parents that at times of great danger you must listen to the animals and birds and trust what they tell you.

CHAPTER 13

UBAYA

"I think there's something over there," I pointed out towards the wooded escarpment. "When it's dark, I'll go and look."

Shola took my arm. "But Mali," she scribbled.

"He's safe with you," I insisted. I was seized with the certainty of what I must do. "I've got to find out what it is before it threatens us. I won't go far, I promise."

"Call me, Leo," she wrote, "every few minutes; the nightjar once, the plover next. If you need help, four calls short and close together."

Together we sat staring ahead of us, and waited for night. We were trying to memorise the shape of the escarpment to help me in the darkness. As dusk fell Shola pointed to a dense clump of trees about a kilometre away. A thin twist of smoke rose at its centre. Fires are illegal in the park. Whoever lit it must have felt confident of their purpose and strength. Now we knew that the danger was human.

I crept down, stealthily, through the bushes and trees of the escarpment. The moon was so bright it almost seemed like daytime. There was now a deathly veil of silence, not even the singing of the tree frogs reached me. I've never been so aware of the smell of the dusty, dry earth. Bats danced silently above me. I was out of breath from the fear of what was drawing closer. I reached the trees.

It was easy to crawl through the thick undergrowth and I was comforted by the camouflage of the bushes. Then, suddenly, I was gripped by the horror of the scene before me. It was like an image from a terrifying film. Four figures sat around a small fire. At first I thought I had stumbled on extraordinary half-human creatures, until I realised the figures before me wore masks. Beautiful dark wooden masks, carved in the shape of deer, impala and birds. But their beauty hid wickedness underneath. Each figure carried a gun and they were talking quickly.

"Is the fencing in place? TELL ME!" said one of them. He spoke with the rough authority of a leader.

"Yes," murmured the others.

"So the elephants are caught in our trap?"

"I have seen them," said another sinister voice. "Many elephants."

"Good, then tomorrow at first light, we start the cull." He gave a short, humourless laugh. "Are the silencers ready?"

"Yes," this time it was a woman's voice.

"Once it is finished, you cut off the tusks and when we've got them loaded, we'll meet up again across the border."

I started to shiver in my hiding place behind the trees. Where did such cold cruelty come from? We had to stop this terrible slaughter. As I moved away, I was too worried for the elephants to look where I was going. Suddenly, a branch snapped under my foot. I froze with fear. I knew they must have heard.

"What was that?" It was the sinister voice again.

"Just a baboon, I expect," laughed another. He reached for his gun and started towards my hiding place. "I'll shoot it."

"No you won't," said the leader sharply. "You'll sit down and save your bullets for the elephants. We don't want Mali on to us."

I was shocked that these menacing masked people could speak of Mali with such familiarity. I called to Shola, the short, hollow whoop of the nightjar. Then I ran back up the escarpment as though the wind itself was blowing me. Shola had come to meet me.

"Is Mali awake, Sho? We need to talk to him." He was, but his face was wrinkled with pain.

"I am disappointed in you," said Mali. "Little Lion, you promised…"

"No Mali, you don't understand. You've got to listen and we must be careful to be silent ourselves now." So I told him and Shola of the strange masked people and of their terrible plan.

"This is very, very bad, Little Lion, but I'm not completely surprised. Akale, one of the rangers, always said that there was one group of poachers left. People lured from our villages by greed and easily led by the promise of money." His fists clenched in anger. "We have our suspicions but no proof. Yes, they are masked so that if rangers ever catch sight of them, their identity remains a secret."

After a few minutes Mali spoke again. "The fence must be at the entrance to the Utenzi Cloud Forest. It is the only logical place. Paula and Elder should bring help very soon. By now they'll be preparing a search party. If nothing else, their lights will scare away this evil group... Maybe we will catch them at last. We must wait. They'll be here with help soon."

And so, we sat down to wait. But I was full of misgivings. Something was wrong. We knew, despite Mali's brave speech, that Paula and Elder should have been here by now. The fate of our beloved elephants lay in the hands of *Ubaya*... evil.

CHAPTER 14

〰〰〰

THE TRAIL

The antelope man, masked and gloating, towered above me.

"*Ubaya! Ubaya!*" he cried, mocking me. I called out and I struggled to get to my feet.

"Sh... sh, Little Lion... it's only a dream." Shola and I had fallen asleep and Mali was awake and watching over us.

He'd pulled himself to a sitting position and leaned against the backpack.

"Mali?"

"Yes, I'm feeling a little better... I can't walk, but I can sit."

"What time is it, Mali?"

"Two o'clock in the morning."

Our instincts were confirmed.

"They're not coming tonight, are they, Mali? Paula and Elder aren't coming."

"I don't think so, Leo. I can only think that they must have decided to return from their relatives in the morning rather than tonight. No one can know we are missing yet."

"But it's all too late, Mali, the poachers start to kill the elephants at dawn."

"Oh Leo," shuddered Mali. "The ground will tremble once more if I cannot prevent another blood bath for our elephants. The evil ones cannot be allowed such a victory, to take the lives of such blessed creatures."

Shola was awake now. She crept over to Mali and placed a finger on his lips. In the light of the lamp she wrote:

Mali,

I know we are still children but we have lived in the wild for longer than these bad poachers. We can use all the things we have been taught to get to this terrible trap and destroy it. Then the elephants will be able to escape to the cover of the forest. We'll be safe in the dark and we'll be back before dawn breaks. The poachers will be sleeping.

Mali started to shake his head.

"Mali, Shola's right, it is our only chance."

"But how can you travel in this darkness?" protested Mali. "Even in daylight it isn't easy."

"When we ran from the rhino, we climbed a tree to look for you. I saw where the elephant trail began again." I pointed up into the night sky. "The moon will light our way. We can follow the trail all the way to the poachers' trap. Mum and Dad would have tried anything to stop them."

"They would," agreed Mali reluctantly. "But I promised them I'd watch over you two. How can I justify risking your lives?"

Shola now wrote:

Aren't we the age you were when you first walked in the bush alone?

"Yes," said Mali, "you are." He sighed and a smile of resignation came to his face.

"Go then. And I'll tell you what my father said to me: I will send out my soul to travel with you and to watch the stars until you return."

This time, as we set out, I felt excitement pump into my beating heart. Shola was ahead of me, walking steadily. We were following the rhino's trail through the open bush. Our tree stood like a reassuring beacon, its silver bark shining in the moonlight.

Shola and I must have sensed the urgency of our mission because suddenly we were both running. Sometimes, in the shadows at our feet, we saw creatures dart across our path. A bush mouse scampered past, calling a warning to its mate.

Just beyond the terminalia tree, the elephant trail began. The meadow turned to dense, rocky bush. I realised why most of our roads had begun as trails cut out by elephants. I pictured them in my mind, the first elephants of Africa, as they made the trail from here all the way to the Utenzi Cloud Forest... before humans came with guns to destroy them.

CHAPTER 15

✕✕✕✕

THE FENCE

It was getting harder to see. The vegetation was thicker on either side of the trail. Something swooped low in front of us and made us jump.

"An owl," I wondered aloud, and then, above the cicadas and in the distance, I heard the rumble of a party of elephants calling to one another. The trail grew steeper. Then we saw a fence loom before us. It cut across the path. Huge, roughly-hewn stumps of wood. They were hammered into the ground and joined together by barbed wire, eight menacing rows of it.

For the first time we felt daunted. How could our pocket knives cut through such terrible wire? What had I imagined we'd do?

"I'll get the torch," I said desperately, "maybe there is a way if we look closer." We crept forward. There was a tremendous crashing of leaves and Shola grabbed my arm. She pulled back into the trees and pointed. A baby elephant came out of the shadows on our side of the fence. It walked in circles and let out a long, resounding cry. Then another elephant appeared on the other side of the fence. Carefully she put her trunk through one of the gaps in the barbed wire and touched the baby elephant. She let out soothing rumbles of reassurance. Then it came to us clearly, this mother elephant was comforting her baby who was marooned on our side of the fence. She could not leave her baby.

In the trees of the forest beyond we could hear rumbles from other members of this family group. Loyal to each other, they would remain close to the mother and baby. This was a scene that even the poachers could not have counted on. They could kill with terrifying ease, taking advantage of the elephants' distress.

Holding the torch we stepped cautiously towards the fence. The mother elephant, picking up our scent, let out a warning bellow. She threw herself against the fence in a desperate but vain attempt to break the barrier between her and her baby. Then she disappeared off into the trees. The baby elephant acted as though it hadn't seen us and continued to pad around in circles of distress next to the wire.

In the torch light we could see that the barbed wire had been bound to the logs with thick twine. We might be able to cut through that. Fumbling nervously I started to cut it, but my hands were shaking so much that the penknife folded and fell into the darkness. Shola found it, and steadying each other's hand, we held the knife together and tried again. The little elephant's anxious, outstretched ears only added to our resolve. At last the first thread in the rope snapped. Then the others followed more easily, or perhaps we just grew fiercer and more determined. We had cut through the twine that bound two of the rows of barbed wire to the stumps. It fell to the ground and I crawled through to the other side of the fence.

I was just standing up, when there was a loud trumpeting call. Advancing through the trees came a larger elephant. Its ears were fanned out. It was charging at us, at me. I tried to roll back under the fence. Then a voice, a voice I thought I would never hear again, screamed aloud.

"IT'S OK, LEO! IT'S LULU."

CHAPTER 16

LULU

A prickling awe crept through me. In that
split second two most astounding things
had happened. Shola had *spoken* and there
before us was Lulu. It was her, we could
see the flower-shaped tear in her ear. Shola
stood still and stretched out her arms.
Lulu stopped. She snorted and flapped her

ears nervously. For a moment I was afraid. Then, very gently, she extended her trunk and traced the outline of Shola's face and then mine.

"Oh Lulu," said Sho softly, in her wonderful, husky voice. "You're *alive*. We didn't dare hope."

"You're back!" I whispered in disbelief, "both of you are back." I wanted to shout it loudly so that it echoed through every lonely corner of the forest. But we both knew there was no time to stop. No time to wonder at the mysterious force that had brought back Lulu and Shola at the same time. The safety of darkness would be gone soon.

"There are others," said Sho, "...on our side. I heard them when we were in the bushes."

"I'll keep cutting, Sho, you give Lulu the gardenia fruit." It was in my backpack and I knew it was her favourite. Sho reached in and laid the fruits on the ground. Lulu scratched her ear and then picked one up and ate it. She picked up another, passed it through the fence and gave it to the baby.

I had not forgotten just how exhilarating it is to stand so close to a wild animal and for them to be unafraid. It is a unique and extraordinary joy. Lulu pulled at the grass and walked backwards and forwards along the fence. She stopped regularly to touch the baby elephant. She snorted and growled and watched us as we hurriedly cut the twine.

As the barbed wire fell to the ground it lay in a twisted and threatening heap. The spikes were fearsome enough to tear at the baby elephant's skin. We needed to pull it clear of the path. I took off my sweater and wound it round my hands to protect them. Shola did the same and we managed to pull the wire clear of three or four stumps.

Lulu made a low call and the little elephant rushed clumsily through the stumps. Lulu's signal must have alerted the mother, who hurried out of the trees. The two were reunited. Rumbling lovingly to each other, the baby hid between the safety of its mother's legs.

"The others won't get through," said Shola, gasping with the effort of pulling the barbed wire. "The gap is still too small between the stumps."

We examined the base of each tree stump with the torch. They seemed indestructible. Then Sho saw that one had been hammered into the soil through soft earth. It had tilted slightly forwards.

"Together," said Shola. "Together if we push…" We turned off the torch. Our eyes took a moment to adjust to the darkness. Then we pushed the stump with every muscle in our bodies until we ached. There was a brief shudder but the stump stood firm.

Lulu was suddenly closer to us. We could feel the soft fanning of her ears and the scent of her body. To our amazement, she laid her trunk against the tree stump. Her tusks gleamed startlingly white. Shola and I stepped out of her way. With a piercing call, as though she had at last identified her enemy, Lulu pushed at the stump. It shuddered obstinately.

And so, repeating her call and with one last tremendous effort, she lunged at the stump. IT FELL. The pathway to safety was opened again.

"Well done, Lulu, oh well done!" crooned Shola lovingly. Lulu stretched out her trunk and touched us on our faces. Then she turned and from out of the cover of the trees came other elephants. They rumbled softly as they followed Lulu through the gap in the fence. Then, like elegant tall ships, they disappeared into the dripping darkness of the forest beyond.

"It's four o'clock, Leo," said Sho. "We've only got one hour 'til dawn. Mali will be waiting." A bubble of joy burst inside both of us and we started to run back along the trail.

Our relief was to be short-lived. Ahead of us we saw lights and dark, looming silhouettes. My ears rang with shock. My hand was numb, we were both trembling as we hid. I remember thinking, "This is it. We're going to die."

CHAPTER 17

THE MORNING STAR

I knew the poachers would be ruthless and unrelenting. They would stop at nothing to kill our elephants. We hid in terror, waiting for their masks to loom above us. I wondered if Lulu and the others had had time to disappear into the forest.

Shola was so restless next to me that I thought they'd see the bushes trembling where we were hiding. Then she whispered, "Let's run for it, Leo. We've got nothing to lose." Her voice crackled with emotion.

"Wait, Sho," I said, clinging to her arm. "If we run through the bushes, they'll think we're the elephants and come after us. It'll give Lulu more time. We're faster than them, I'm sure. When we get to the bush we'll lose them."

I heard a strange voice and torch light swept the trail. Our path was blind but when I looked up, I could just see the morning star already high in the sky.

"Ready, Leo," said Sho. "I'll count to three."

I groped in the darkness. It was like balancing on the edge of a cliff. There was no going back.

"One, two, three, go…" hissed Shola.

We crashed and rattled the trees. Seized by an intrepid force we ran faster. I wonder if we even remembered to breathe.

Then a shower of seed pods fell on me and up ahead I heard a muffled cry. Shola had fallen. I stumbled next to her and to my horror a strong beam of torch light caught us in its glare. I crouched by Sho, shielding us.

"*Ondoka*! Leave us alone!" I cried.

"Leave us!"

The awful truth of our situation hit me.

"Who are you? How can you do this?" shouted Shola, catching her breath and sobbing with frustration.

"*Mtoto*," said a gentle voice. "A child."

"Wait," another said.

"IT'S THEM, IT'S SHOLA AND LEO. Oh, thank heavens we've found you!" It was Paula and Elder with two other rangers.

"Paula?" cried Shola in amazement.

"Shola! Yes it is, BUT YOU CAN SPEAK…. HOW? Oh this is wonderful. Lower the torch, Elder, they can't see us. Tatu, TATU, they're HERE!" Paula, who was normally calm and quiet, was stuttering with excitement. To awake from the nightmare of our situation into Paula's loving arms was so extraordinary that I couldn't stop shaking. We sat for a moment and tried to understand what had happened.

"We got back after midnight," said Paula. "We had a puncture… you weren't there. The radio wouldn't pick you up. We knew something was wrong, so we came looking for you straightaway."

"Shola, say something else!" said Tatu. "I can't believe it."

"Nor can I," said Shola, beaming. "But look! We've got no time, there are the first red streaks of light. We must stop them before it's too late… there are poachers."

"They said they would set off at first light," I explained. "I heard them. They'll kill all of the elephants. Lulu's new family have gone into the Utenzi Cloud Forest… But they haven't had time to get far… We thought you were the poachers…"

"Ssh Shola, Leo, it's OK. Mali told us about them but you were our priority. The other two, Mabiti and Ubula, who were here a minute ago, have gone to meet three other rangers to ambush the poachers."

"If we hurry," said Tatu, "we might see them captured!"

We sat by Mali, all three of us dazed by lack of sleep, silent witnesses to the strangest Bakuli dawn I have ever seen. Everywhere lay still until one gunshot sounded out. It was as if it signalled the passing of danger. For even before we knew for certain that the ruthless group had been captured, a chorus of birds started to sing in glorious rhythm. Impala and zebra emerged from the shadows, and far off an elephant called.

It was as though nature had gathered to celebrate as evil was marched out of their sacred valley. The poachers, still wearing their masks, emerged from the trees. Their heads were bowed. They would be taken to the local police.

"It's over," said Mali, leaning back again on his makeshift pillow. "We have them all now at long last. And we have you to thank, my brave cubs. I am very proud. Your parents would be too."

"They are," said Shola. Her eyes filled with tears. "They are, I feel them now, Leo. You were right, they are always with us now and it took me all this time to feel them watching over us."

CHAPTER 18

A NEW BEGINNING

Shola, Tatu and I were sitting on the porch steps in our pyjamas. Sho was hugging Daisy and picking fleas out of her fur.

Paula came out to us and Elder was with her. She carried a lamp which she hung from the porch above us. We all went quiet, there was something conspiratorial about Paula tonight.

"Ma's got something to say," said Tatu.

"I have, yes," her voice had a strange nervous lilt to it. She swallowed.

"Shola and Leo, I must tell you a story. When Tatu was born, Elder's mother, Nona, told me he should be called 'Tatu'. As you know, this is the Swahili word for the number three. I remember Elder translating this for me, and me asking her 'Why three?' She answered, 'Because he is to be one of three.' We couldn't have any more children and I always wondered why she had been so certain. Today it became clear to me. When we found you both in the forest, I realised suddenly how I loved you as my own."

"Yes, I felt so too," smiled Elder, suddenly shy.

"Later," continued Paula, "when Tatu asked us if we could adopt you as his brother and sister, Nona's words, 'one of three', echoed in my ears. So, Shola and Leo, if you would agree to it, we would love you to be part of our family always. We know we can never replace your parents, but we could be your guardians and your home would always be with us."

We had been through so many feelings in so few days, Shola and I did not even need to look at each other. We both kissed Paula and Elder and said "yes" terribly quickly. Then we ran down the porch steps into the garden. Tatu was chasing Teddy in circles.

"I've got a brother and sister now, Ted," he was saying, and laughing. Soon we were chasing Ted as well until we fell in a heap of dust, happiness and bare feet.

As always it took Mrs B. to put some shape into all the events of the past few days.

"Let me see! I must get this straight," she said as we stood by her desk the following morning. "Leo returns, Shola speaks, Paula and Elder and Tatu are to have a large family and our village is rid of terrible poachers. WELL, we cannot possibly carry on without a celebration! There are just too many wonderful events for us all to concentrate on our lessons. We need to dance and sing to absorb it all."

So school work was cancelled and we all set to work to prepare a party. I cannot ever remember another moment such as this. Lilac and red flowers scattered the schoolroom floor, Paula and Elder cooked delicious food on a barbecue and we wore our traditional African dress of plum red cloth and bright beaded jewellery. Mrs B. was in charge of the music. Mali, his leg in plaster, was the conductor. There cannot be anything on earth so exhilarating as being part of the harmony of voices and drums. We ate, sang and danced for what seemed an eternity of dizzy joy.

SHOLA'S WORDS: A POSTSCRIPT

Paula once said that each soul finds its rightful home. I cannot remember anything about the time before you, except that I had never felt love before. Sometimes in my sleep I see places that I feel I've been to, but never people.

When Mama and Baba died, and you were taken away, I thought it was the end. It was as though someone closed a lid tightly over me. My voice was wrenched from me. Until then I hadn't ever thought about our differences. I was convinced that as I was African and you were English, and because I had never been adopted by Mama and Baba, that we would be separated for ever. Now I know that where spirits and hearts are joined together, no one can divide them. Seeing Lulu in the Utenzi Cloud Forest unlocked my voice. It was Lulu and Sala who brought me first to my family here, and once again it was them who brought me back to you.

Nearly two years have passed. You and I are now Tatu's brother and sister. It is written in print as well as in our hearts.

Yesterday evening we went to the Wimbo to swim. I was ahead, looking for grasses to wind into a headdress for my banana-leaf angel. I looked up.

"Leo, Tatu, come quick. Look!" I whispered. To our amazement, through the trees, came a procession we'd given up hope of ever seeing again. It was Lulu and her family of elephants. They had come to drink and play at the river. It was the first time they had come this far since the poaching began. At last their confidence and trust had come back.

With the elephants' return we knew that our world, which had been turned upside down, could now return to the way it had been when our families had shared their lives together. Lulu, Leo and I are no longer alone.